Just the right angel

The archangel pulled a book out of the folds of her gown and flipped through the pages. "Yes, here it is. Oh, little angel, have I got a treat for you."

"What?" The Little Angel of Imagination closed up his tray of paints and turned to the archangel expectantly.

"Someone who needs help badly. And you're just the right angel to give it."

"A lot of help?" asked the little angel. "Enough to earn the rest of my feathers?"

"Absolutely," said the archangel.

"Can I choose the kind of bell that will ring when I get my wings?" asked the Little Angel of Imagination. "Because if I can, I want the bell that rings at the beginning of a horse race."

The archangel laughed. "We'll see, little angel. We'll see."

Aladdin
Angelwings
No. 8

Playing Games

Donna Jo Napoli
illustrations by Lauren Klementz-Harte

Aladdin Paperbacks
New York London Toronto Sydney Singapore

For Mamma,
with all my love

Thank you to all my family,
Brenda Bowen, Cylin Busby,
Nöelle Paffett-Lugassy, Karen Riskin,
and Richard Tchen

First Aladdin Paperbacks edition April 2000

Text copyright © 2000 by Donna Jo Napoli
Illustrations copyright © 2000 by Lauren Klementz-Harte

Aladdin Paperbacks
An imprint of Simon & Schuster
Children's Publishing Division
1230 Avenue of the Americas
New York, NY 10020

Library of Congress Cataloging-in-Publication Data
Napoli, Donna Jo, 1948–
Playing games / Donna Jo Napoli. — 1st Aladdin Paperbacks ed.
p.   cm. — (Aladdin Angelwings ; 8)
Summary: The Little Angel of Imagination is assigned to Louie, a boy who
has forgotten to use his imagination, and tries to help him rediscover how
to open up his mind as he plays with his dog and his little brother.
ISBN 0-689-83208-7 (pbk.)
[1. Angels—Fiction. 2. Imagination—Fiction. 3. Brothers—Fiction.
4. Dogs—Fiction.]
I. Title. II. Series, Donna Jo, 1948–   Aladdin Angelwings ; 8.
PZ7.N15Pl   2000   [Fic]—dc21   99-87418   CIP   AC

Angel Talk

The Little Angel of Imagination dipped his brush in black paint and made a circle, leaving a small point of white in the center. He added lashes.

The Archangel of Imagination came up beside him. "What a beautiful eye. What kind of animal will it be?"

"A horse. I'm painting a horse race."

"Really? I didn't know you like horses."

"I don't like them, I love them," said the Little Angel of Imagination. "My favorite pastime is hanging around the farms where they train racehorses." The little angel used brown to fill in the rest of the horse's head around that shining eye. Long, slender legs pounded the earth. A thick mane and tail trailed in the wind. Finally, he turned

and searched through his paints. "Oh, no."

"What's the matter?"

"I don't have the right color for the grass."

The archangel smiled. "Skip the grass. Just put in a lot of palm trees."

"But there aren't any palm trees at this racetrack."

"So what? It would look great. And you could add those cactuses with the yellow flowers and . . ."

"No way," said the little angel. "I'm painting a particular race. The Kentucky Derby. And the grass has to be blue-green."

"Well, how about that aquamarine over there? That looks just like the sea."

"But the grass in Kentucky isn't like the sea." The little angel threw down his brush. "This is so frustrating."

"Relax. No one will care if you make the grass a slightly different color from how it really is."

"I'll care. Everything has to be just right.

3

This is the most important horse race ever. And now I can't paint it. I've got to find something else to do."

The Archangel of Imagination picked up the paintbrush and carefully cleaned it in the jar of water. She held it out to the little angel.

The little angel took it without looking her in the face. "That was stupid of me. I got carried away because horses are so wonderful." He dried the brush with a soft cloth.

"Hmmm. That reminds me . . . " The archangel pulled a book out of the folds of her gown and flipped through the pages. "Yes, here it is. Oh, little angel, have I got a treat for you."

"What?" The Little Angel of Imagination closed up his tray of paints and turned to the archangel expectantly.

"Someone who needs help badly. And you're just the right angel to give it."

"A lot of help?" asked the little angel. "Enough to earn the rest of my feathers?"

"Absolutely," said the archangel.

"Can I choose the kind of bell that will ring when I get my wings?" asked the Little Angel of Imagination. "Because if I can, I want the bell that rings at the beginning of a horse race."

The archangel laughed. "We'll see, little angel. We'll see."

TV

"Louie!"

Louie didn't look up from the TV. He stayed super quiet, hoping Mamma wouldn't figure out where he was.

"Louie!" Mamma called again. He heard her footsteps.

Louie got up off the couch and ran for the stairs. If he shut himself in the bathroom, no one would bother him. Then he could go back down to the TV once Mamma had given up on him.

Mamma beat him to the stairs. "Didn't you hear the phone ring?"

"Sure."

"Why didn't you answer it, then? I was busy and by the time I got to the phone, they'd hung up."

"Next time, answer faster," said Louie.

"Louie, it's almost always for you."

"No it isn't."

"It used to be." Mamma looked thoughtful. "Why don't you call someone and go play?"

"I don't want to play."

"You're getting addicted to that TV."

Louie didn't answer. It was true. So what?

"Please, honey. You've got to get outside and have fun."

"TV is fun."

"What's fun about it?"

"I always know what the characters are going to do."

"That's fun? That's boring," said Mamma.

"For you, maybe. I like it."

Mamma's shoulders slumped. She looked sad. "Will you please go call Sean? Do it for me, okay?"

Louie went into the kitchen. His little brother, Willard, was kneeling on a chair, mashing up bananas in a bowl. Willard grinned at Louie. Louie picked up the receiver and dialed.

"Hello." It was Sean.

"Hi," said Louie. "What's up?"

"I'm getting some guys together for D and D." Sean hesitated. Finally, he asked, "Want to play?"

"I'm busy," said Louie.

"Okay."

"Bye," said Louie. He hung up.

"That was rude, Louie," said Mamma.

"No it wasn't."

"Poor Sean. You call him up, then you say you're busy. You never see him anymore."

"He didn't really want to play with me," said Louie.

"What a thing to say. He's your best friend."

"Sean likes role-playing games. You know, like Dungeons and Dragons."

"What's that?"

"He makes up adventures and quests and junk I'm not good at."

Mamma laughed. "How can you not be good at a game?"

Mamma had no idea. Sean made up wild,

dangerous adventures, and Louie just ruined the whole game by having the character do something stupid and ordinary like break an arm. Louie could never think of anything exciting. "I like TV." He walked out of the kitchen to the family room.

Mamma followed him and caught him by the arm. "Listen, Louie, you've been sitting in front of this TV all morning. You even ate your lunch here. That's enough. You're going to play with Willard now."

"Willard?" Louie almost fell backward in shock.

Mamma made a little *tsk*. "I've got to take your grandmother to the beauty parlor this afternoon, and we have guests coming to dinner, and . . ."

"Who's coming to dinner?" Louie asked in alarm. "You didn't invite those people with the mean kids again, did you?"

"The Fords. And their kids aren't mean. They're just a little . . . I don't know . . . exuberant."

"I hate them."

Mamma screwed up her mouth. "Well, maybe this time you'll like them. Anyway, I need you to play with Willard while I work on dinner for a while."

"If you cook dinner now, it'll be cold and rotten by the time everyone gets here," said Louie. "On the other hand, then maybe they'll never come again."

"Don't be a wise guy. I have to chop things and make the dessert and, well, you know, Louie. Just help me, okay?"

"I'll chop things. You play with Willard."

"Louie, you need to play. Come on."

"I hate playing with Willard, Mamma."

"You seem to hate everything today."

"No I don't. But I can't play with Willard. What can I play with a three-year-old?"

"He's almost four."

"I'm a zillion times older than him."

"That's not true. Anyway, this is a ridiculous conversation. You're going to play with

Willard so that I can get some things done, and that's that."

"I have to go to the bathroom."

"Well, hurry up. I need you." Mamma kissed Louie on the cheek. "Look, I don't know why you've gotten into this TV thing, but it needs to be in moderation. You've spent every weekend on that couch for the past couple of months."

"It's not like a disease, Mamma. It's not going to kill me."

"Maybe not, but it's not doing anything good for you, either. Playing is good for you."

"How?" said Louie.

"I don't want an argument. I've got to have your help right now. Just a couple of hours."

"You don't really need me. A moment ago you were encouraging me to go off and play with Sean. Now you're saying you need me just because you think it's good for me to play."

"I do need you, Louie. Your father had to go into the office today, and there's no one else to help me. Please," Mamma whispered.

"Oh, all right." Louie sighed and followed Mamma back into the kitchen. He looked at Willard.

Willard grinned at Louie.

"Why do you always grin at me, Willard?"

"I love you."

"Oh." Louie loved Willard, too. He just didn't want to play with him. "All right. We have to play. What do you want to do, Willard?"

"Cook."

Louie looked at Mamma. "He should help you, Mamma."

Mamma took an odd-looking vegetable out of the refrigerator. "You two go play somewhere. Somewhere besides the kitchen."

"Come on, Willard, let's go upstairs to your room."

"No." Willard climbed off the chair and ran out the back door.

"Mamma," said Louie.

"Hurry up," said Mamma. "Scoot."

Angel Talk

"I'm not the Little Angel of Friendship or the Little Angel of Patience," said the Little Angel of Imagination. "I'm just me. Louie has too many problems for one angel."

"Are you having a crisis of confidence?" asked the Archangel of Imagination.

"No. But I can only help with imagination." The little angel took out his sketch pad and drew the outline of Louie's face.

"Somehow Louie has lost his imagination; that's his problem. Why do you think he doesn't want to play with his brother?" asked the archangel.

"Little brothers can be annoying," said the Little Angel of Imagination, filling in Louie's hair on the drawing.

"What about not wanting to play with his friend?"

"Maybe he's going through a shy stage," said the little angel. He erased Louie's nose— it was too small.

"Really? Do you remember the reason he gave his mother for not playing with Sean?"

"He said Sean likes role-playing games, and he's not good at them," said the little angel. He put down his pencil. "Ah, I see: Role-playing games take a lot of imagination. Maybe you're right. But playing with a little brother doesn't take imagination."

"Oh, doesn't it?" The Archangel of Imagination gave a small smile. "How long has it been since you played with a little kid?"

"Too long," said the little angel slowly.

"I know what you mean." The Archangel of Imagination looked wistful for a moment.

"Are you sure this is really a job for me?" asked the Little Angel of Imagination. "His mother seems to be working on him pretty good. Maybe she'll do everything that should be done."

"I think you can add a lot. And, besides, I think you'll have fun on this job. After all, you did say you like horses, didn't you?"

"This has something to do with horses?" The Little Angel of Imagination smiled wide. "When do we get to the horse part?"

"Now."

Stewball

Willard ran straight for the doghouse. The dog was sleeping behind it in the shade of the huge old tree, like always. "Wake up, Stewball." Willard leaned over Stewball and shouted in her ear. "Time to play."

The dog opened her eyes and looked groggily at Willard.

Louie got on his knees and searched around under the bushes. "Here's the soccer ball."

"I can't play soccer," said Willard.

"Stewball can." Louie kicked the ball.

Stewball ran scrambling after it.

Willard clapped his hands and laughed.

Louie played with Stewball till the old dog collapsed in a heap.

"My turn," said Willard. He straddled Stewball.

The dog groaned.

"What are you doing?" Louie dribbled the ball in a circle.

"I'm riding her." Willard bounced high. "Get up, doggie. Gallop."

"Dogs don't gallop." Louie balanced the ball on top of his toes, then flipped it straight up. When it came down, he butted it with his head.

"Stewball's a horse," said Willard.

"She's a dog."

"She's a horse," said Willard. "She gallops."

"Oh, yeah? Stay right here." Louie ran to the back door and peeked in the kitchen. Mamma was on the phone and she was writing something on a pad of paper. Louie tiptoed inside, opened the freezer, took an ice-cream sandwich, and tiptoed back outside.

Willard was waiting for him at the door, eyes huge.

Louie walked over to Stewball. "Here, girl,

smell this." He unwrapped the ice cream and held it in front of Stewball's nose.

Stewball opened one eye. She sniffed hard.

Louie held the ice cream higher.

Stewball stood up and ate the ice-cream sandwich.

"She's up," said Louie. "Let's see you try to gallop her."

Willard grabbed a huge clump of Stewball's hair in each hand and thrashed his legs around until he managed to get all the way onto her back.

The dog wobbled and sat down.

Willard slid off.

"Willard," called Mamma from the window. "Don't sit on Stewball."

"I'm riding her," said Willard.

"People can't ride dogs. Stewball isn't big enough."

"I told you," said Louie.

"Feed her more ice cream," called Willard.

"Ice cream?" Mamma came to the back

door. "Louie, is that what you got when you snuck into the kitchen?"

"Huh?" Louie dribbled the soccer ball all around Willard. "Why'd you tell on me?" he said out of the side of his mouth.

"Ice cream, ice cream," called Willard. "Feed Stewball and she'll get big. Then I can ride her." He hugged Stewball.

Mamma walked out into the yard and picked up the ice-cream wrapper. "Louie, did you feed the dog an ice-cream sandwich?"

"She needed it," said Louie. He kicked the ball against the side of the garage.

"Louie, don't break a window. And I don't buy ice-cream sandwiches so you can feed them to the dog."

"She liked it," said Willard.

"That doesn't matter," said Mamma. "Ice cream is people food. Dogs eat dog food." She gave Stewball a scratch behind the ears. "Good old dog."

"Good old horse," said Willard.

"That's why I can't play with Willard, Mamma. He's doesn't know anything. He thinks Stewball's a horse."

"Willard, no matter what, you can't sit on Stewball, and Louie . . . " Mamma turned to Louie with an open mouth. Then she shook her head. "I'm in a rush. Just play."

Angel Talk

ou were right about Louie's problems," said the Little Angel of Imagination. "But this doesn't have anything to do with horses."

"Not real horses, no," said the archangel. "But I'm sure you don't have any trouble imagining the horse inside that dog."

"Actually, a dog isn't all that much like a horse," said the little angel. "Horses have hooves, and their tails are long strands of hair, and their heads . . . "

"Wait a minute," said the Archangel of Imagination. "Are you telling me you can't pretend a dog is a horse?"

"Well, when you put it that way, sure, I can pretend. But Louie obviously can't."

"So help him," said the Archangel of Imagination.

23

"No," said the little angel. "Stewball can't even carry Willard around. The last thing we need is for Louie to start seeing the dog as a horse and for him to climb on, too. He'd crush the dog."

"Then you have to find another solution."

"The perfect solution." The Little Angel of Imagination rubbed at a paint stain on his hand. "I'll do my best."

The Sandbox

"Go play in your sandbox," said Louie.

Willard grinned. He ran to the sandbox and dug happily.

Louie kicked the soccer ball against the side of the garage.

"Louie, I told you not to do that," Mamma called from the kitchen window. "You'll break a window. Go play with Willard in the sandbox."

If you're so rushed, Louie thought, how do you have time to spy on me? He dribbled the ball over to the sandbox. "What are you making, Willard?"

Willard looked up and grinned. "A horse-food bowl." He ran to the bottom of the oak tree. He came back with both hands full, and dumped leaves and twigs and acorns into the sand bowl. "Here, Stewball. Eat."

25

Stewball lifted her head and looked lazily toward the sandbox.

"Here, Stewball," Willard called again in the same tone Mamma used when she called Stewball to dinner.

Stewball stood up and walked over. She looked at the mess in the sandbox and walked away.

"Dogs won't eat leaves and junk like that," said Louie. He went to kick the sand bowl, but as he drew back his foot, it stuck there in midair, as though someone were holding it. "What?" He wiggled his ankle until his foot felt okay. Then he looked again at the sand bowl. "When I was little, I used to dig all the time," he said.

"What did you make?" asked Willard.

Louie got on his knees and dug a deep hole. He made a high wall all around it.

"Oh, it's big," said Willard. "Now it's a real horse-food bowl."

"No, it's not," said Louie. "It's a wishing well."

"What's a wishing well?"

"You close your eyes and throw in a coin and make a wish."

"I don't have a coin," said Willard.

"Then you can't . . . " Louie's mouth was stuck open, as though something were jammed into both sides. He couldn't talk. He massaged the corners of his mouth till it felt normal again. "When I was little, I used pebbles for money."

"I got pebbles." Willard ran to the driveway and came back with two handfuls of pebbles. He closed his eyes and threw them into the wishing well. "I wish . . . "

"You can't say it out loud," said Louie quickly. "You have to wish silently. Inside your head. Just like wishing with candles on your birthday."

Willard stood there with his eyes closed. He squinched up his face. Then his eyes shot open, and he ran to Stewball. He stood over the sleeping dog. He stood there a long time.

Finally, Louie walked up behind Willard. He rubbed his hands on his jeans to get the sand off. "What are you doing?"

"Waiting."

"I can see that," said Louie. "What for?"

"I'm going to be first."

"Huh? What are you talking about?"

"Stewball's going to be a horse. And I'm going to be first to ride her."

Louie tilted his head. "You poor kid. You really are crazy."

Angel Talk

"id you grab his foot?" asked the Archangel of Imagination.

"Yup. I stood behind him." The Little Angel of Imagination pointed to a red spot on his shin. "I was standing so close, I got kicked."

"And did you do something to his mouth?"

The Little Angel of Imagination held out his hand. Teeth marks crossed the top.

"That must have hurt," said the archangel.

"It was worth it. I stopped him from saying Willard couldn't make a wish because he didn't have a coin."

"That's a blessing," said the Archangel of Imagination. "No little kid should be told that wishes depend on money."

The little angel nodded. "And each time I stopped Louie, it gave him a moment to think

it over and remember what he used to do when he was little. That's good, too, right?"

"Right," said the archangel. "But physically restraining him has its problems. You'd better come up with something else fast, or you're going to need bandages."

The little angel laughed and gingerly touched the teeth marks on the back of his hand. "I'll see what I can do."

The Grocery

"Louie, Willard, I have to go grocery shopping." Mamma beckoned them in.

"Shopping, shopping," chanted Willard, marching into the kitchen. "I love shopping."

"How can anyone love shopping?" said Louie.

"Come on, Louie, don't be such a grump. You used to love going to the grocery with me when you were little." Mamma washed off the counter and put the milk, eggs, and butter back in the refrigerator.

"Go have a good time, then," said Louie, heading off for the TV.

"Come." Willard grabbed the hem of Louie's shirt. "You come, too."

"I've got things to do."

"Come with me," wailed Willard.

"Mamma, get him off me."

Willard let go of Louie's shirt. "I'll stay with Louie."

"Uh-uh," said Mamma. "You're coming shopping with me."

"No," said Willard.

"You love shopping, remember?"

"I want Louie."

"Louie's coming, too," said Mamma.

"What?" Louie glared at Mamma. "That's not fair."

"I only have a couple of last-minute things to get. I'll be quick. And you have to take care of him for a while longer when we get home, anyway, so what does it matter?" Mamma slung her purse over her shoulder. "Let's go."

"Mamma . . . "

"Right now."

Willard sat in the metal seat of the cart and swung his legs. Mamma was comparing prices on cans in the foreign foods aisle. "Louie," said Willard.

Louie looked down to read the ingredients on a can of lobster bisque. "Hmmm?"

"Catch me," said Willard.

Louie looked up in time to see Willard, who was now standing in the seat, take a giant step out. He grabbed him around the chest, and they both fell, Willard on top of Louie.

"What're you boys doing?" Mamma rushed over.

"I want to walk," said Willard. "Louie's taking me."

Louie shook his head, but somehow he couldn't open his mouth to talk. He could hardly even breathe.

"Well, all right," said Mamma, straightening Willard's shirt. "But I only have a few more things to get. So meet me at the checkout counter in fifteen minutes." She threw a can into the cart and pushed it down the aisle.

Louie gasped for breath as air finally filled his lungs again.

"Come," said Willard. He ran off.

Louie caught up with him. "Where're you going?"

"You have to hold me up."

"What? Up where?"

"Come." Willard ran to the meat section and stood in front of the butcher's window. "Ring the bell."

"You want to talk to the butcher?"

"Yes."

"What'll you say to him?"

"Ring the bell."

"Don't be stupid, Willard. He'll get mad if we ring the bell for no reason."

"Ring the bell," shouted Willard.

A woman searching through the steaks glanced at them and gave Louie a frown.

"Don't shout," whispered Louie. Then, as if by magic, his hand lifted up, and he rang the bell.

The butcher opened the window. "What can I do for you?"

"Me," said Willard. "Me. Hold me up, Louie."

"You can talk loud enough from there," said Louie.

"Please." Willard hopped in place.

"Oh, all right."

"Is there something I can do for you?" asked the butcher.

"I want horse food," said Willard.

"Horse? We don't sell horse here." The butcher closed the window and went away.

Willard looked at Louie. "Ring the bell again."

"No. Listen, Willard, he didn't even know what you were talking about because your question was so stupid."

Willard's face crumpled in that way Louie knew too well.

"Don't cry," said Louie. "It doesn't help to ask the butcher. Horses don't eat meat."

"What do they eat?" asked Willard.

"Carrots, apples, things like that."

"Stewball doesn't like those things."

"Stewball?" Louie shook his head. "I thought you were asking about horses."

37

"I am. What else do horses eat?" asked Willard.

Louie shrugged. "Well, grains."

"Where's the grain window?" asked Willard.

"There is no grain window. Grains are in everything. Bread and spaghetti and cookies and . . . "

"Cookies," said Willard. "Let's feed Stewball cookies. Then she can grow into a horse."

Louie took Willard by the hand. "You are one sorry little crazy person," he said. "That won't work. But at least we can get some good cookies."

They picked Oreo cookies and Fig Newtons and Chips Ahoy! and ran to meet Mamma at the checkout.

"Cookies?" said Mamma. "I already picked out a box of graham crackers. That's a much better snack."

"Cookies," said Willard.

Louie smiled at Mamma. "You heard him." He dumped the cookie boxes into the cart.

Angel Talk

Watch out," said the archangel. "You almost smothered him."

"I didn't mean to. I just put my hands over his nose and mouth for a moment."

"And then you lifted his hand and made him ring the bell." The Archangel of Imagination shook her head. "I know you're working hard to help Louie. But if you do things like that, he's going to think he's losing control of himself."

"He isn't worried yet," said the little angel. "He has so little imagination, he just accepts everything that happens to him."

"Exactly. So that's the problem you have to focus on: opening his mind, not restraining his body. Louie's got to choose to use his imagination. You can't force it on him."

The Little Angel of Imagination made a fist of his right hand and lightly punched it into his left palm. "This kid is such a tough case. But I'm going to find a way. And I'm going to find it without holding him back anymore."

"Go for it."

Fig Newtons

"We'll help put things away," said Louie.

Mamma smiled happily. "What a nice offer. Thank you, boys. Then I can get right back to work on dinner." She carried a bag of lettuce to the sink and washed it.

Willard took the cookie boxes out of the grocery bags one by one and handed them to Louie, who stacked them in the cupboard. When Willard handed him the Fig Newtons, he tucked them under his shirt, putting his finger to his lips to hush Willard. "Let's go out back, Willard," he said loudly, so that Mamma would hear.

They ran out the door.

Willard went straight to Stewball. "Get ready, doggie." He jumped in place.

Stewball opened her eyes.

Louie ripped the top off the box of Fig Newtons. He jammed one in his mouth and handed one to Willard.

Willard jammed it in his mouth and held out his hand. "For Stewball," he mumbled as he chewed.

Louie gave Willard another cookie.

Willard held the cookie over Stewball's nose, just like Louie had held the ice-cream sandwich.

Stewball's nose twitched. She lifted her head and ate the cookie in one gulp.

Willard watched her. "She doesn't look any bigger."

"I told you," said Louie, biting into another Fig Newton. "She needs more."

Louie handed Willard another cookie.

Stewball stood up.

Willard put the cookie in Stewball's mouth. "She still doesn't look bigger."

"What'd I say?"

"She needs more cookies."

"We shouldn't waste them," said Louie.

"Give me some."

"No."

Willard grabbed at the box of cookies, and the front side ripped off. A long stack of Fig Newtons fell on the ground.

Stewball gobbled them up fast, making lots of smacking noises as she tried to clean the sticky fruit off her teeth. Then she looked eagerly at Louie.

"Forget it." Louie clutched the rest of the cookies to his chest.

"She's growing," said Willard.

"No she isn't," said Louie.

"Look at her legs."

Louie looked closely at Stewball's legs. "I don't see anything."

"They're longer. Like a horse's legs." Willard wrestled his way onto Stewball's back.

Stewball lay down.

"Fig Newtons aren't doing anything," said Louie.

"Let's try the Chips Ahoy!"

"We can't," said Louie.

"Why not?"

"I forgot to tell you," Louie said, looking away. He lowered his voice. "Dogs can't eat chocolate."

"What? Why not?"

Louie mumbled, "It's bad for them."

"Can horses eat chocolate?"

"I don't know."

"Then let's feed her Oreo cookies."

"Don't be dumb. Oreo cookies have chocolate, too," said Louie.

"What? Then we have nothing else to feed her." Willard looked at Louie. "You're mean."

"It's not my fault."

"You knew dogs can't eat chocolate." Willard threw himself over Stewball's neck in despair.

Angel Talk

*I*s it true that dogs can't eat chocolate?" asked the little angel.

"I'm not sure, but I think so," said the
Archangel of Imagination.

"Then Louie did do a really mean thing to
Willard." The Little Angel of Imagination got
hot with anger. "He got Willard to make
Mamma buy the cookies he wanted to eat, not
the cookies that would make Stewball grow
into a horse."

"Wait a minute," said the archangel. "Listen
to what you just said. You're not actually think-
ing that a dog can change into a horse, are you?"

"Oh." The Little Angel of Imagination gave
a small shrug. "Of course not. I guess I got carried away again." Then he rubbed his palms
together. "Ha! If I could get carried away like

that, I bet Louie could, too. And he deserves a little shaking up."

The archangel cocked her head. "What do you mean?"

"You'll see."

Ears and Tail

"I'm sorry, Willard," said Louie gently. "But, really, it doesn't matter how many cookies you would have fed her. Stewball's a dog and she'll never be a horse."

"How do you know?" Willard sobbed. "Her ears were just starting to change."

Louie got down on one knee. "Her ears are like they've always been, Willard."

Stewball's ears stood up for a second, then they flopped back down. The dog tilted her head, as if she was confused.

Louie blinked. He petted Stewball.

Stewball's ears stood up again.

Louie dropped his head forward and gaped.

Stewball's ears flopped back down.

Louie looked at Willard, but Willard's face

was buried in the dog's hair; he hadn't seen Stewball's ears stand up.

Louie petted the dog's ears. Then he held up the tips. The dog looked quizzically at him.

Willard turned his head to face Louie. "What are you doing?"

"I thought Stewball did something funny with her ears."

"She did?" Willard put his face right in front of Louie's. "See? Let's feed her more Fig Newtons. Fast."

Louie handed two cookies to Willard.

Willard laid them on the ground in front of Stewball.

Stewball stood up and snarfed down the cookies. Then she lay back down and licked at her teeth. Suddenly her tail stuck straight out behind her. Stewball jerked her head up and looked quickly back over her shoulder.

"What's going on?" said Louie.

"She's a horse," said Willard.

"That's impossible." Louie sat down and crossed his legs.

Willard sat beside him.

The boys stared at the dog.

Angel Talk

he Archangel of Imagination doubled over with laughter. When she finally straightened up, she put her hand on the little angel's shoulder. "Good trick."

"Thank you."

"But you're not planning on walking around behind that dog all day long, holding out her tail and ears, are you?"

"No," said the little angel. "I just wanted to give Louie a little shock."

"Well, you certainly did that. He's staring at Stewball as though he expects her to start whinnying any moment."

The Little Angel of Imagination whinnied himself and pawed at the air with his arms.

"What are you doing now?"

"I can't figure out what to do next, so I'm

trying to think like a horse. If I can imagine every detail of a horse's life, maybe an idea will come."

"Sometimes the details don't have to fit," said the archangel.

"Yes they do. The details are very important," said the Little Angel of Imagination. "If the details are wrong, nothing you make up seems real."

"Is it working?" called the archangel as the little angel galloped by.

"I think so."

A Break

"Nothing's happening," said Louie.

"Let's feed her bread."

"Stewball won't eat bread."

"She has to," said Willard. "You said grains are in bread, so she has to eat bread or she won't grow into a horse."

"Stewball hates bread."

"We need better grain. And we don't have any." Willard slumped forward, with his elbows on his knees. "I'll never ride a horse." His voice cracked.

Louie put his arm around his little brother's shoulders. "Don't be so sad."

Willard sighed loudly.

Louie remembered unpacking the groceries. "Let's go get the graham crackers Mamma bought."

"Are graham crackers grain?"

"Yup."

Willard grinned and ran into the house. Louie followed.

"Good. You're just in time," said Mamma. "I'm ready to take Grandma to the beauty parlor. So you're off duty, Louie. Willard's coming with me."

"I don't want to come with you," said Willard. "I have to feed Stewball."

"Stewball doesn't eat in the middle of the day." Mamma put on her sunglasses. "Come on."

"Stewball *needs* graham crackers," screamed Willard.

"Don't shout, Willard." Mamma looked at Louie. "Are you the one behind feeding the dog all these things?"

"Me?" said Louie.

"Yeah, you. You fed her the ice-cream sandwich."

Louie didn't say anything.

"Well, no more odd food for the dog," said Mamma.

"She needs grains," moaned Willard.

"Grains?" Mamma took Willard by the hand. "We'll talk about this later. We can't make Grandma late." She pulled Willard down the hall and out the front door.

Louie headed straight for the TV. He grabbed the remote control as he sank onto the couch. He surfed the channels. All the good shows were over already. But that didn't matter. The afternoon was full of great reruns. He settled on one and let himself relax.

The couch was soft, and pretty soon Louie felt drowsy. He laid his head back on the cushions. His eyes slowly closed.

"Neigh!"

Louie sat upright. He looked around the room. Then he laughed at himself. The horse was on TV, of course. Where else could it be? But, hey, this wasn't the channel he had chosen. This was some old Western. He must have pressed on the remote control by accident when he was settling into the cushions. He switched back to the other channel and leaned back. A different show now, but another rerun. Before long, he was dozing again.

Ba rum ba rum ba rum.

Louie jumped up. A horse galloped across the screen. He'd done it again. He would have to put the remote control on top of the TV so he couldn't press on it by accident anymore. But first he'd switch back to his channel.

Except this movie looked okay after all, so who cared? Some sheriff got off his horse and tied it to a tree. The horse immediately started grazing on the grass. Louie watched thoughtfully.

Louie switched off the TV. He got up and went outside. Stewball was sleeping in the shade, of course. Louie ripped up a handful of grass and held it to the dog's nose.

Stewball sniffed and opened her eyes. She wagged her tail lazily, then closed her eyes again.

"You don't eat grass, do you, Stewball?"

Stewball opened her eyes and licked at her teeth.

"Are those figs still bothering you?" Louie petted her back firmly, the way she liked it. "What happened to your ears before?"

Stewball's tail thumped.

"And to your tail?" Louie petted Stewball slowly now. "You know what? I used to ride you. Do you remember?"

Stewball rolled onto her back.

Louie rubbed her belly. "I just remembered. You were a lot younger then, but you still used to sit down when I'd climb on you, too. You're a smart dog."

Stewball barked.

"Don't worry, old girl. You're the best dog there is. You don't have to be a horse."

Louie went back into the kitchen, through the house, and out to the front porch. He sat on the steps and waited.

Angel Talk

Something's up," said the Little Angel of Imagination. "What's he doing?"

"I don't know," said the archangel. "But at least he's not watching TV anymore."

"You're right. Hey, maybe he's actually waiting for his brother. When Willard gets home, I bet he's going to play with him."

"That's what I think, too," said the archangel. "Only what will they play?"

"Louie will think of something."

"And if he doesn't," said the archangel, "I'm sure you'll help him."

"That's my plan."

Animal Crackers

Willard jumped out of the car. "Let's get the graham crackers," he said as he ran past Louie into the house.

Louie ran behind Willard into the kitchen.

"Hurry," said Willard.

"Willard, graham crackers won't . . . "

"Hurry up! Before Mamma comes."

Louie opened the cupboard. Maybe they could build houses out of graham crackers. And if that didn't work, at least they could eat them. He picked up the box. Behind it was another box—of animal crackers. Pictures of lions and elephants and zebras stared out at Louie. "Willard, what is it about riding a horse that's so special?"

"It's fast."

"Is that all?" asked Louie.

59

"And it's high. You sit up high."

Louie smiled. "I've got an idea."

"Willard?" called Mamma. "Where are you?"

"He's with me," Louie called back. "We're busy."

"What?"

"We'll be in the backyard," called Louie. He grabbed the box of animal crackers, and they ran outside.

Willard went straight to Stewball.

"Forget Stewball," said Louie. "She'll never be anything but a dog."

Willard's face fell. "But you said . . . "

"I've got something better. Come on." Louie went over to the picnic table. "How would you like to ride a zebra?"

"I love zebras," said Willard.

Louie opened the box of animal crackers and dumped them on the picnic table. "Okay, separate out all the zebra ones."

Willard stood on the bench, and together

the boys made a pile of zebra crackers.

"Now feed them to me," said Louie.

"To you?"

"Do it," said Louie.

Willard put a zebra cracker in Louie's mouth.

Louie ate it. He threw back his head and stroked his ears. "See how long my ears are growing? Zebra ears." He opened his mouth.

Willard carefully placed another zebra cracker on Louie's tongue.

Louie ate it. He sat on the bench and stretched out both arms and both legs. He swung them around. "I'm growing zebra hooves." He opened his mouth.

Willard dropped in two zebra crackers at once.

Louie stood up, turned around, and shook his bottom at Willard. "I've got a thick, bushy tail."

Willard laughed. "Zebra tail."

Stewball came over and sat by the bench,

her eyes on the animal crackers.

Willard put the rest of the zebra crackers in Louie's mouth.

Louie munched them all down. "That's it! I can feel it all over." He made a loud, high noise through his nose and trotted around the picnic table.

Stewball trotted after him, nipping playfully at his heels.

Louie sidled up to the bench. "Climb on if you dare."

Willard screamed in delight. He climbed on Louie's back and put his legs around his waist and his arms around his neck.

"Just don't strangle me," said Louie. He hooked his arms under Willard's knees and galloped around the yard as fast and as high as he could.

Stewball barked and barked.

Angel Talk

"Did you put those animal crackers in the cupboard?" asked the Archangel of Imagination.

"Nope. I just moved them so they were right behind the graham crackers."

"Well, that was a brilliant move."

"Thanks." The Little Angel of Imagination put his hands in his pockets and tried not to appear too cocky. "Louie's doing good. He should have gotten on all fours, though. A zebra doesn't gallop only on his hind legs, after all."

"They're having a lot of fun," said the archangel.

"I know."

"So maybe some details don't have to be just right, after all."

The little angel watched the brothers.

Willard was laughing as Louie jumped pretend fences. "You're right. I guess my job is done, then."

"Don't be so fast," said the archangel. "A lot of what has happened so far came from Willard's ideas and your strategic moves. But you're not finished until Louie is able to come up with some ideas of his own, without help."

The Little Angel of Imagination jumped with the thrill of anticipation. "I bet he can already. And I can't wait to see."

Guests

Louie reached for a slice of watermelon.

"Wait," said Mamma. "Louie, why don't you carry the bowl of watermelon into the backyard and all you boys can play together as you eat dessert."

Louie looked at his mother, but she avoided his eyes. He didn't want to play out of earshot of the adults, where the boys who were visiting could do mean things with no one to stop them.

"Go on." Mamma picked up the bowl and handed it to Louie. It was amazing that she could do that without looking at him at all.

Louie carried the bowl through the kitchen and out to the picnic table.

The bigger boy, Jeff, grabbed a slice of watermelon, took a bite, and spit seeds all over. "Did you see that? I bet I can spit seeds farther than you."

His little brother, Thomas, took a slice and spit seeds. They splattered down his shirtfront.

Willard laughed.

"What are you laughing at?" Jeff took another bite. Then he spit watermelon seeds in Willard's face.

"Hey, don't do that!" Louie jumped in front of Willard.

Stewball came bounding over. She barked.

"Keep that mangy dog away," said Jeff.

"Yeah," said Thomas. He climbed up on the picnic table.

"Stewball's good," said Willard, wiping the seeds off his forehead. "She never bites."

"Is that so?" Jeff took another bite. This time he spit watermelon seeds on Stewball.

Stewball sneezed.

"That's it," said Louie. "I didn't want to have to do this, but you forced me." He put his hand in his pocket.

"What've you got there?" said Jeff, backing up.

Louie took out four lion crackers. He handed two to Willard. "Let's do it, Willard." He ate his two lion crackers.

Willard looked confused for a moment. Then he grinned. "Oh, I get it." He ate a lion cracker. Then he turned around and fed the other one to Stewball.

Louie roared.

Willard roared.

Stewball howled.

"You're nuts," said Jeff.

Louie stalked around to the other side of the picnic table. Willard stalked behind him. Stewball tagged at their heels.

"They're lions!" screamed Thomas.

Louie held out a lion cracker toward Thomas. "It's your choice. You're either a lion or lion meat."

Thomas snatched the cracker and ate it. He leaped off the table and stalked with

Louie and Willard and Stewball.

"What about me?" said Jeff.

Louie felt in his pocket. "There's still one lion cracker left."

"Are there any other kinds?"

"Elephants."

"Lions can't kill elephants," said Jeff.

"They can if they gang up on him," said Louie.

"Be an elephant, Jeff," said Thomas. "Please. Otherwise we have no one to gang up on."

"I don't want to be the only elephant," whined Jeff.

"I can call my friend Sean to be an elephant with you," said Louie.

"Okay," said Jeff. "Feed me."

Louie fed Jeff an elephant cracker.

Jeff gave a loud elephant trumpet.

The kitchen door opened. Mrs. Ford stood there and waved. Her bracelet jingle-jangled. "Are you boys okay?"

"Stay out of the jungle, Mom." Jeff went lumbering off behind the tree.

Thomas and Willard and Stewball all huddled together, planning their attack, while Louie ran into the house to call Sean.

Angel Thoughts

The newest Archangel of Imagination flew up to his easel on his strong, wide wings. He had all his feathers now, and it wasn't the loud bell at the start of a horse race that had rung to announce him earning his wings, it was the simple little bell on Mrs. Ford's charm bracelet. He laughed.

The horse in his painting was running fast and furious, as sleek as any animal could be. The newest archangel picked up the paint-brush and dipped it in the white paint. He made a high wall with broad, sweeping strokes. Now no one could see the grass behind it. They'd have to use their imagination to envision the blue-green Kentucky grass. That was a cheat, sort of. But it would be good for people to exercise their imaginations that way.

Still, the newest archangel could help out a bit by stimulating their sense of color. He rinsed his brush, then dipped it in blue. He painted a vine full of flowers hanging heavy over the wall. And now he dipped his brush in pine green and painted a forest in the distance. Then something large and furry coming through the trees.

This wasn't the Kentucky Derby at all. His beautiful horse was shining with the sweat of a real race. This horse had a mission. The newest archangel dipped his brush in another color, letting his imagination lead him.

How to Draw a Horse

1. Use light lines to start your drawing.

2. Draw the largest oval– the horse's body–in the center of your page.

3. Following the diagram above, lightly sketch the dotted lines (circles, cones, and ovals).

4. Use your imagination to fill in the horse's face, mane, tail, and hooves. What color will your horse be?

Don't miss these other
Aladdin *Angelwings* stories:

No. 9

Lies and Lemons

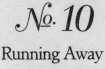

No. 10

Running Away

No. 11

Know-It-All